LARGE PRINT

Christmas Stories

Brown Watson

ENGLAND

Polar Penguin's Theme Park

It was the first day of the Christmas holiday.
"I'm bored!" said Flapper.
"Nothing to do!" groaned Flipper.
"Is it Christmas yet?" asked Flupper.
Flop was busy thinking. He'd had an idea.
But he would need some help from his
friends.

"What's a theme park?" asked Flupper when he saw Flop's sign.
"Rides and slides," said Flop, "Come with me!"
Archie Albatross was waiting for them.

POLAR PENGUIN'S THEME PARK

"Climb on board and sit tight for AirAlba," he said. They soared over frozen lands, icebergs and ice-blue seas. "Wow! What a view!" cried Flipper.

Next, Flop took them to the biggest, scariest iceberg.

"Get ready for the Numb Bum Slide," he cried.

"Whoosh!" They went bombing down.

"Splash!" They landed in the water.

They tried it on their tummies. And they whizzed down on their bottoms.

"And again," cried Flapper.

"Me too!" said Flipper.

But the fun didn't stop there.
"Hold on tight," said Watty Whale.

The polar penguins shot up on a jet of water, bounced onto Watty's back and clung on as he dipped and dived in the waves. Little Squirt's Fountain of Fun was the best ride yet!

Finally, the penguins were worn out. "Time for a story, I think," said Flop. They gathered around Wendy Walrus who knitted them a good yarn!

None of the penguins were bored now. Every day of the holiday they had fun at the Polar Theme Park.

"What day is it tomorrow?" asked Flupper one bedtime.

"I don't know," said Flapper.

"Me neither," said Flipper.

"IT'S CHRISTMAS DAY!" said Flop.

And they all fell about laughing.

How could they forget?

It was a good job Santa hadn't.

13

Teddy Finds a Home

Teddy lived in a very hot country. The sun shone all year round. Even at Christmas time it was warm enough to sit on the beach.

Teddy had lots of friends he could play with. But the thing he wanted most of all was someone to belong to; someone to be his special friend.

One Christmas Eve, Santa came to the store in Teddy's town.

"What would you like for Christmas?" Santa asked Teddy.

"I'd like to belong to a family," said Teddy.

"That's easy!" laughed Santa. "I know just the one. Hop in this gift box and I'll take you on a sleigh ride."

Later that night, Santa delivered Teddy to his new home. He peered out of his box. There were three children tucked up in bed.

"My new family," thought Teddy, excitedly.

The next morning Teddy was greeted by excited squeals.

A pair of chubby hands lifted him up and a pair of beautiful eyes looked at him lovingly.

"I so wanted a teddy!" said a little girl with curly hair.

Teddy was just as pleased to meet her too!

A Dog for Christmas

Biscuit was a very happy dog.
The Clark family had bought him for their
daughter, Lucy, for Christmas. He was well
fed and everyone made a fuss of him.

One day, a robin was singing in the garden. "Come and play!" he trilled. "Come and play!"
Biscuit wasn't really allowed out on his own but he did want to go and play.

Before he knew it, Biscuit had
bounded out of the house.
"Hello," he said to the robin.
"Hello," said the robin.
"Would you like to play a game?"
"Yes please," said Biscuit.

The robin showed Biscuit where all the rabbits were hiding.

They smelt very good to Biscuit. He was off! He chased them over snowy slopes and through pine-scented forests.

But he was only a little dog and they always got away from him.

Back at the house, Lucy was getting
worried.
"It's getting dark," she told her dad.
"I wonder where Biscuit has got to."
"Don't worry," said Dad.
"I'm sure he'll come back
when he's ready."

Just then, there was a scratching at the door.
Biscuit was home again!
"You bad dog," said Lucy, but gave him a
big hug.
Biscuit was sorry he had
upset her. He decided
he wouldn't run
off on his
own again.

The Sleepy Elf

The elves were very busy at the Toyland workshop.

Teeny was testing a toy car. "Vroom, vroom, VROOOM!"

Tiny was sorting through letters to Santa. "Shuffle, shuffle, shuffle."

Trim, Slim and Thin were decorating
the sleigh. "Tinkle, tinkle, tinkle."
Weeny was making a wooden toy.
"Tap. Tap. Tap."
He loved his job but today his head hurt.
And he could hardly keep his eyes open.
He was so tired.

"I think I'll just lie here for a minute," he thought to himself.

Vroom, Vroom! Shuffle, Shuffle! Tinkle, Tinkle! ... But there was no Tap, Tap. Weeny had fallen fast asleep.

Santa Claus came over to the workshop. When he saw Weeny asleep on the floor he picked him up and carried him home. "Oh dear!" he said. "I think my elves have been working too hard!"

A few hours later Weeny woke up.
He couldn't hear Vroom, Vroom!
Shuffle, Shuffle! Tinkle, Tinkle.
Instead he could hear the other
elves laughing and having fun.

He ran to the window and Santa waved to him. "You have all been working so hard, I thought you needed a holiday," said Santa. "Come and join in the fun, Weeny." And that's exactly what he did.

33

Little Duck's Surprise

Dinky Duck was very excited. This Christmas was the first year she was allowed to stay up to see Santa.

"What's Santa like?" she asked Mr Cow, as her brother, Doug handed him a present.
"He wears a blue hoodie and orange slippers," said Mr Cow.

"What's Santa like?" she asked Mr Donkey, as she handed him a pretty pink package. "Cow got it all wrong," said Donkey. "Santa wears dark glasses and drives a limousine."

Dinky's older brother, Dan, had a long parcel for Mother Hen.

"What's Santa like?" Dinky asked the busy mum.

"Donkey was being silly," said Mother Hen. "Everyone knows Santa rides a camel and wears a top hat."

It was getting dark by the time the Duck family had given out all their presents.
They hurried along to the special place to watch for Santa. All the other animals were there too.
Dinky was very excited.

The stars came out one by one. Everything was still. The sound of bells jingling broke the silence.

"He's here!" cried Mrs Duck and looked up. All the other animals looked up too.

Then Dinky looked up. "No one told me he could fly!" she gasped as she saw Santa swoop across the sky in his splendid sleigh. It was a magical moment; much better than she could ever have imagined.

Grandpa's Christmas Day

It was nearly Christmas. Santa's elves had filled lots and lots of sacks with presents. But Santa still had some lists from grandpas to read out.

"Socks and toffees for Grandpa George," said Santa. The elves filled a sack.

"And marmalade and slippers for Grandpa Arthur." The elves filled another sack. "Ah ha! What have we here?" asked Santa, his eyes lighting up. "Grandpa Ted has asked for a bright orange coat and a shiny purple skateboard!"

On Christmas Eve, William hung up one stocking for him and one for his sister, Poppy.

"What about you, Grandpa?" asked William.

"Maybe I'm a bit too old to be getting presents," said Grandpa Ted.

But then he remembered the letter he'd sent Santa.

"You never know," he thought to himself and hung his stocking up too.

What a surprise they had in the morning! All the stockings were bulging, including Grandpa's!

He ran to the fireplace, pulled down his stocking and tipped his presents on the floor.

"Wow!" he cried when he saw the shiny purple skateboard and bright orange coat.

"I'm going out to play right now!"

"Weeeee!" Grandpa shouted from his skateboard. "I haven't had this much fun in years."

He whizzed down the hill, crashed into the hedge and fell into a snowdrift.

But he got up and had another go.

He played all morning.

After lunch Grandpa Ted put his feet up and fell asleep.

"I love Grandpa," said Poppy softly, "but he's not like other grandpas, is he?"

"No," said William grinning, "he's much more fun!"

The Fairy Ball

Every Christmas, Fennel sat on top of the Christmas tree. She didn't mind it up there. But she liked it best of all when Polly fell asleep. Then Fennel came alive.

Most nights she just flew around the room.
But tonight she flew right out of the window!
"I'm so happeee!" she cried as she danced
and twirled in the cold night air.

"Twitt t-wooo!
Who are you?"
asked an owl who was sitting on
the branch of a tree.
"I'm Fennel. And I just love
Christmas, don't you?" she laughed.
And she slid down an icicle into a big
snowdrift.

Just then she met Flori and Fern.
"Hi Fennel! Coming to our party?" they
asked her.
"Ooo! Yes please," Fennel replied.
The fairy ball began. There was music
and dancing, heaps of food and a lot of
fairy giggles.

Suddenly Fennel realised the time.
"Quick! I have to get back before midnight,"
she said, "before I become just an ordinary
fairy again."
"Doe Deer will take you," said Flori.

They sped through the night and Fennel was
back just in time.
But who was that
on the roof?

"You're up late Little One," said Santa.
"I've been to the best party ever," sighed Fennel.
And with that she twirled on the spot, fluttered her wings and flew back into the bedroom.

Little Donkey

Little Donkey was tired. He had been plodding along for hours now. The ground was rough and stony. His legs hurt and his back ached. But still he kept going. "Clip, clop... clip, clop... clip, clop."

At last he could see the lights of Bethlehem twinkling in the distance.

Mary leant over and stroked his head. "Not far now," she whispered. "Then we can all have a rest."
Her voice was so warm and soft Donkey forgot to be tired. He had a feeling that something very special was about to happen.

At last they arrived in Bethlehem. Mary led Donkey through the bustling crowds and busy streets. "Poor Donkey," she said. "You must be very tired. I hope we find somewhere soon."

Joseph knocked on the door of one inn after another. But the reply was always the same:

"No room! No room!"

Then Donkey spotted the stable. It looked warm and cosy. He whinnied and nudged Joseph to let him know that here was a place they could stay.

"We've no room here, I'm afraid," said the innkeeper. "But it looks like your donkey has found you somewhere."

62

Later that night Donkey woke up. Mary had given birth to a baby boy. She laid him gently in the hay, right next to Donkey.

Some shepherds arrived to see Jesus. "Angels sang to us and told us where we would find him," they said. As time passed by, everyone fell asleep. But Donkey kept watch over the baby all night. What a wonderful night it had been.

The Jolly Snowman

"Look Charlie! It's snowing!" cried Lucy when she opened the curtains on Christmas Eve. Snowflakes were swirling past the window, the garden was white and the branches were weighed down with snow.

"Let's make the jolliest snowman we can," said Charlie.

So they did. They gave him Grandma's floppy hat and mum's multi-coloured scarf.

"He does look very happy," said Lucy, smiling. "Let's call him Jolly."

Jolly was a very happy snowman. He giggled when a snowflake landed on his nose. He laughed at the robin who circled his head. And he beamed at the children when they said goodnight that evening.

But then night came. The sky was dark. The garden was dark. Jolly gave a shiver. His smile faded and he covered his face.

"What's wrong?" asked a passing bunny.

"I'm afraid of the dark!" wailed Jolly.

Suddenly, Jolly heard a sound in the distance like bells tinkling. It got closer and closer. It was so beautiful Jolly forgot to be afraid. He opened one eye and then the other. Santa had arrived!

"Happy Christmas, Jolly," said Santa and handed Jolly a present. It was a torch. Jolly switched it on and light flooded the garden. "Thank you!" said Jolly. "It's just what I've always wanted." And he gave a huge beaming smile.

Santa's Little Helpers

"I don't know what to do," Santa told Scott Seagull. "All the reindeer are ill. Who will pull the sleigh now?"

"My penguin friends are good at helping out," said Scott. "The only trouble is they can't fly."

But that wasn't a problem to Santa.
He taught them to fly in no time at all.
Soon they were gliding and
swooping in the air as if
they'd always done it.
"Whoopee! We can fly!"
they cried.

That evening Santa loaded the sleigh until it was overflowing with presents.

"Let's go, team!" he shouted.

And they were off, the cold night air rushing past them and snowflakes dancing before their eyes.

Delivering the presents was so much fun.
One by one the penguins slithered down
the chimney: first Flipper, then Flapper,
Flupper and Flop! But filling the stockings
wasn't quite so easy.

"I think I'm going to sneeze," said Flop in a loud whisper.

"Ssshh!" warned Flipper.

But it was too late. "Ahh, Ahh TCHOO!" Flop's sneeze rang out. They peered at the boy. He was still fast asleep!